An Illustrated Timeline of

DINOSAURS

by Patricia Wooster
illustrated by Len Epstein

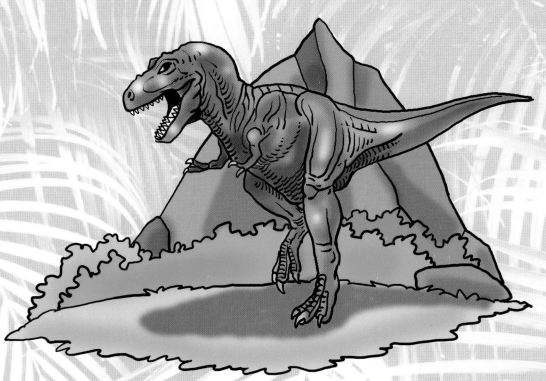

PICTURE WINDOW BOOKS
a capstone imprint

Special thanks to our adviser for his expertise, research, and advice:
Mathew J. Wedel, PhD
Paleontologist and Assistant Professor
Western University of Health Sciences, Pomona, California

Editor: Shelly Lyons
Designer: Lori Bye
Art Director: Nathan Gassman
Production Specialist: Danielle Ceminsky
The illustrations in this book were created digitally.

Photo Credits: Shutterstock: Andrea Danti, Diana Rich

Picture Window Books
1710 Roe Crest Drive
North Mankato, MN 56003
www.capstonepub.com

All books published by Picture Window Books
are manufactured with paper containing at least
10 percent post-consumer waste.

Library of Congress Cataloging-in-Publication Data
Wooster, Patricia.
  An illustrated timeline of dinosaurs / by Patricia Wooster ;
illustrated by Len Epstein.
     p. cm. — (Visual timelines in history)
  Includes index.
ISBN 978-1-4048-7162-5 (library binding)
ISBN 978-1-4048-7253-0 (paperback)
  1. Dinosaurs—Juvenile literature. I. Epstein, Len, ill. II. Title.
  QE861.5.W68 2013
  567.902'02—dc23
                    2011029063

Printed in the United States of America in North Mankato, Minnesota.
102011   006405CGS12

Have you ever wondered what the world was like during the more than 165 million years dinosaurs roamed Earth? You're not alone! Dinosaurs have captured our imaginations for many years.

Great fossil discoveries have given us clues about these fascinating animals. This book is your guide to learning about dinosaurs. You can follow the events in order, or jump back and forth on the timeline. We've broken up this book into eras and periods, so it's easy to move around and explore. From a dinosaur the size of your hand, to one that stands more than six stories tall, you're in for an exciting adventure!

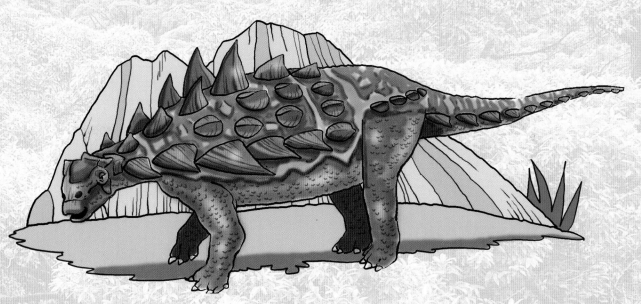

Editor's note: Because dinosaurs lived so long ago, scientists don't know everything about them. In this book, a question mark (?) represents a fact that is unknown or is scientists' best guess.

PALEOZOIC ERA
(542 MYA–251 MYA)

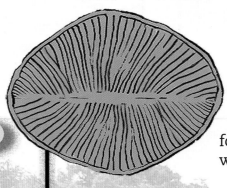

fossil of a
worm or polyp

542 million years ago (mya)

The largest explosion of
animal life begins. Dozens of
new species appear on Earth.

440 mya

A mass extinction takes place.
Fossils show that about
60 percent of life dies out.

542–488 mya

The first animals with bony skeletons,
called vertebrates, show up on Earth.

488–443 mya

Thousands of new sea
creatures, such as the first
modern-looking corals and
mollusks, appear.

359–299 mya

Eggs with shells and protective membranes develop. Animals can now lay eggs on land.

251 mya

Less than 10 percent of all animals survive the largest mass extinction in history. Scientists think volcanic activity, climate change, or an asteroid hitting Earth may have caused the extinction.

375 mya

The first vertebrates emerge from water and walk on land.

300 mya

Anapsids appear. They are the first reptiles on Earth.

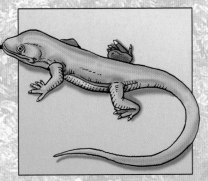

270 mya

The supercontinent Pangea is fully formed. It covers about one-third of Earth's surface.

TRIASSIC PERIOD
(250 MYA–200 MYA)

228 mya

Eoraptor (EE-oh-RAP-tore)
Family: ?
Fossils Found: Argentina
Diet: Omnivore
Length: 3 feet (0.9 m)
Fact: Eoraptor is thought
to be one of the first dinosaurs.

230 mya

Flying reptiles called Pterosaurs live
on Earth. They have no feathers.
Instead they have fur or hair.

240 mya

Nothosaurs swim the seas.
They look like dinosaurs
but are actually reptiles.

227–221 mya

Staurikosaurus (store-IK-oh-SORE-us)
Family: Staurikosauridae
Fossils Found: Brazil
Diet: Carnivore
Length: 7 feet (2.1 m)
Fact: This dinosaur is longer
than an adult human but
weighs just 65 pounds (29 kg).

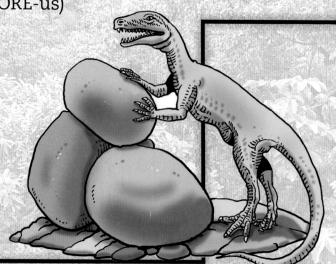

225 mya

Herrerasaurus (huh-RARE-ah-SORE-us)
Family: Herrerasauridae
Fossils Found: Argentina
Diet: Carnivore
Length: 17 feet (5.2 m)
Fact: Herrerasaurus weighs more than 400 pounds (181 kg). That's as much as a male lion.

228–199 mya

The supercontinent, Pangea, begins breaking apart.

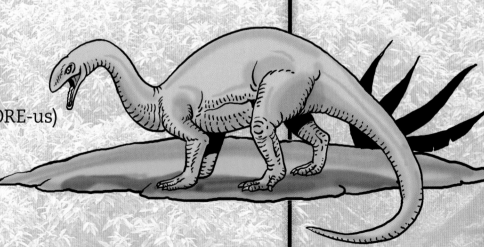

227–205 mya

Thecodontosaurus (THEE-koh-DON-tuh-SORE-us)
Family: Thecodontosauridae
Fossils Found: England and Wales
Diet: Herbivore; Length: 10 feet (3 m)
Fact: Thecodontosaurus has teeth that fit into spaces in its opposite jaw.

TRIASSIC PERIOD
(250 MYA–200 MYA CONTINUED)

221 mya
Warm-blooded animals that produce milk first appear. They are called mammals.

220 mya

Chindesaurus (CHIN-dee-SORE-us)
Family: Herrerasauridae?
Fossils Found: United States
Diet: Carnivore
Length: 6.5 feet (2 m)
Fact: Chindesaurus' long whiplike tail may be used for balance.

221–210 mya

Riojasaurus (REE-oh-hah-SORE-us)
Family: Melanorosauridae
Fossils Found: Argentina
Diet: Herbivore; Length: 36 feet (11 m)
Fact: In 1969, a nearly complete Riojasaurus skeleton is found in Argentina.

221–210 mya

Antetonitrus (ant-EE-toe-NYE-trus)
Family: ?
Fossils Found: South Africa
Diet: Herbivore
Length: 33 feet (10 m)
Fact: Antetonitrus lashes out at predators with a clawed thumb.

220-200 mya

Coelophysis (seel-OH-fye-sis)
Family: Coelophysidae
Fossils Found: United States
Diet: Carnivore; Length: Less than 9 feet (2.7 m)
Fact: Coelophysis has large eyes that
may be used for night hunting.

210 mya

Plateosaurus (PLAT-ee-oh-SORE-us)
Family: Plateosauridae
Fossils Found: Northern and Central Europe
Diet: Herbivore
Length: 23 feet (7 m)
Fact: Plateosaurus weighs
as much as 4 tons (3.6 t).
That's more than the average
weight of two cars!

215 mya

Mussaurus (moo-SORE-us)
Family: Plateosauridae
Fossils Found: Argentina
Diet: Herbivore
Length: 10 feet (3 m)?
Fact: Only hatchling Mussaurus fossils
have been found. At just 9 inches (23 cm)
long, the fossils are the smallest nearly
full dinosaur skeletons ever found.

TRIASSIC PERIOD
(250 MYA–200 MYA CONTINUED)

▶ **208–204 mya**

Massospondylus (mass-oh-SPON-dih-lus)
Family: Massospondylidae
Fossils Found: South Africa and
United States
Diet: Herbivore; Length: 13 feet (4 m)
Fact: Massospondylus swallows small stones
to grind food in its stomach.

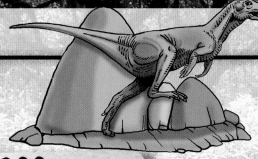

208–200 mya

Heterodontosaurus
(HET-er-oh-DOHNT-oh-SORE-us)
Family: Heterodontosauridae
Fossils Found: South Africa
Diet: Herbivore; Length: 50 inches (1.3 m)
Fact: Heterodontosaurus has three
different kinds of teeth. It can bite,
tear, and grind its food.

208–194 mya

Scelidosaurus (skel-EYE-doh-SORE-us)
Family: Scelidosauridae
Fossils Found: England and United States
Diet: Herbivore; Length: 10–13 feet (3–4 m)
Fact: Scelidosaurus is the first large
armored dinosaur.

208–188 mya

Barapasaurus (bar-rap-oh-SORE-us)
Family: Vulcanodontidae
Fossils Found: India
Diet: Herbivore
Length: 60 feet (18 m)
Fact: Barapasaurus has legs and feet similar to those of modern-day elephants.

205–202 mya

Scutellosaurus
(skoo-TELL-oh-SORE-us)
Family: ?
Fossils Found: United States
Diet: Herbivore; Length: 4 feet (1.2 m)
Fact: Scutellosaurus' bony studs protect it from predators.

200 mya

Major climate changes take place. The changes cause more than 50 percent of all living things to go extinct.

205–202 mya

Vulcanodon (vul-KAN-oh-don)
Family: Vulcanodontidae
Fossils Found: Zimbabwe
Diet: Herbivore
Length: 20 feet (6.1 m)
Fact: Vulcanodon is named after the volcanic rock where it was first discovered.

JURASSIC PERIOD (199–146 MYA)

170-160 mya

Cetiosaurus (see-TEE-oh-SORE-us)
Family: Cetiosauridae
Fossils Found: England and Morocco
Diet: Herbivore; Length: Up to 60 feet (18 m)
Fact: Cetiosaurus, a bulky bodied dinosaur, walks on four legs.

190 mya

Anchisaurus (an-chih-SORE-us)
Family: Anchisauridae
Fossils Found: United States
Diet: Herbivore; Length: 7 feet (2.1 m)
Fact: Anchisaurus fossils are first discovered in 1818. The bones aren't described as dinosaur bones until 1885.

199 mya

Large dinosaurs start to become the main land creatures.

190 mya

Dilophosaurus
(die-LOAF-oh-SORE-us)
Family: Coelophysidae
Fossils Found: United States
Diet: Carnivore; Length: 20 feet (6.1 m)
Fact: *Dilophosaurus* means "two-crest lizard."

170-160 mya

Shunosaurus (SHOON-oh-SORE-us)
Family: Cetiosauridae
Fossils Found: China
Diet: Herbivore
Length: 40 feet (12 m)
Fact: Shunosaurus has a bony club at the end of its tail. It most likely uses the club to fend off predators.

170-155 mya

Megalosaurus (MEG-ah-low-SORE-us)
Family: Megalosauridae
Fossils Found: England
Diet: Carnivore; Length: 30 feet (9.1 m)
Fact: Uncovered in England in 1676, Megalosaurus is the first dinosaur fossil to be named.

157-154 mya

Tuojiangosaurus (too-HWANG-oh-SORE-us)
Family: Stegosauridae
Fossils Found: China
Diet: Herbivore
Length: 23 feet (7 m)
Fact: Tuojiangosaurus has 15 pairs of spines running down its neck, back, and tail. The spines may be used for defense.

170–160 mya

Gasosaurus (gas-uh-SORE-us)
Family: ?
Fossils Found: China
Diet: Carnivore
Length: 13 feet (4 m)
Fact: Gasosaurus is named "gas lizard" in honor of the gas company that found its remains.

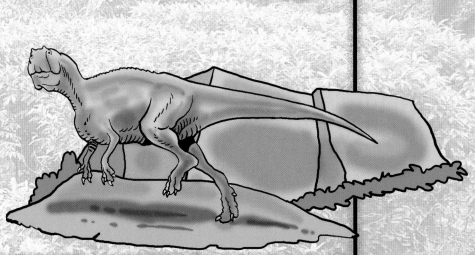

JURASSIC PERIOD
(199–146 MYA CONTINUED)

155–145 mya

Diplodocus (dih-PLOH-duh-kus)
Family: Diplodocidae
Fossils Found: United States
Diet: Herbivore
Length: 90 feet (27 m)
Fact: Diplodocus has a 26-foot-long (8-m-long) neck. From nose to tail, this dinosaur is longer than a tennis court.

155–140 mya

Brachiosaurus
(BRAK-ee-uh-SORE-us)
Family: Brachiosauridae
Fossils Found: United States
Diet: Herbivore
Length: 85 feet (26 m)
Fact: Brachiosaurus is about 50 feet (15 m) tall. It probably has a strong heart that pumps blood all the way up its neck to its head and brain.

155 mya
The first bird, Archeopteryx, looks a lot like a dinosaur. It has a long tail and jaws with teeth.

155–144 mya

Stegosaurus (STEG-uh-SORE-us)
Family: Stegosauridae
Fossils Found: United States and Portugal
Diet: Herbivore; Length: 28 feet (8.5 m)
Fact: Although this dinosaur is as big as a school bus, its brain is as small as a walnut.

155-145 mya

Barosaurus (BARE-uh-SORE-us)
Family: Diplodocidae
Fossils Found: United States and East Africa
Diet: Herbivore; Length: 66–88 feet (20–27 m)
Fact: Barosaurus looks a lot like Diplodocus, but its neck is much longer.

154-145 mya

Apatosaurus (ah-PAT-uh-SORE-us)
Family: Diplodocidae
Fossils Found: United States
Diet: Herbivore
Length: 70–90 feet (21–27 m)
Fact: Weighing 38 tons (34 t), Apatosaurus is one of the largest land animals ever to live. Its footprint can be 3 feet (0.9 m) wide!

155-135 mya

Allosaurus (AL-uh-SORE-us)
Family: Allosauridae
Fossils Found: United States
Diet: Carnivore; Length: 40 feet (12 m)
Fact: Allosaurus has bony ridges above its eyes. They may have been used to attract mates.

150-140 mya

Camarasaurus (KAM-uh-ruh-SORE-us)
Family: Camarasauridae
Fossils Found: United States
Diet: Herbivore; Length: 75 feet (23 m)
Fact: Camarasaurus is named for the air spaces in its backbone.

CRETACEOUS PERIOD
(145–65 MYA)

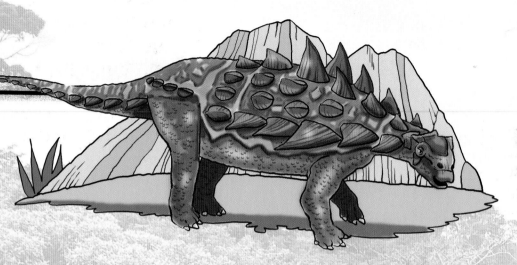

142-127 mya

Gastonia (gas-TOE-nee-ah)
Family: Ankylosauridae
Fossils Found: United States
Diet: Herbivore
Length: 16 feet (4.9 m)
Fact: Gastonia's long spikes make it difficult for predators to attack.

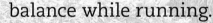

125 mya

Hypsilophodon (hip-sih-LOH-fuh-don)
Family: Hypsilophodontidae
Fossils Found: Europe
Diet: Herbivore; Length: 6.5 feet (2 m)
Fact: Hypsilophodon has a stiff tail that helps the dinosaur keep its balance while running.

140-110 mya

Iguanodon (ig-WHAHN-uh-don)
Family: Iguanodontidae
Fossils Found: England, Belgium, Germany, North Africa, and United States
Diet: Herbivore; Length: 30 feet (9.1 m)
Fact: Coal miners in Belgium will find more than 20 skeletons of Iguanodon. For this reason, Iguanodon becomes a popular dinosaur to study.

125 mya

Baryonyx (bare-ree-ON-icks)
Family: Spinosauridae
Fossils Found: England
Diet: Carnivore; Length: 33 feet (10 m)
Fact: Baryonyx has large thumb claws that may help it catch fish.

121-112 mya

Minmi (MIN-mee)
Family: Nodosauridae
Fossils Found: Australia
Diet: Herbivore; Length: 10 feet (3 m)
Fact: Minmi has an unusually small head. Scientists believe the animal was not very smart.

121-112 mya

Suchomimus (sook-oh-MIME-us)
Family: Spinosauridae
Fossils Found: Niger
Diet: Carnivore; Length: Up to 36 feet (11 m)
Fact: Suchomimus has hooked teeth with which it easily grasps and pierces fish.

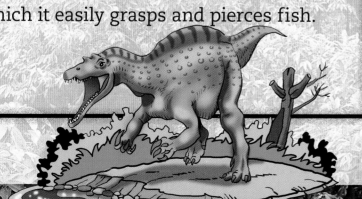

120-110 mya

Deinonychus (die-NON-ih-kus)
Family: Dromaeosauridae
Fossils Found: United States
Diet: Carnivore; Length: 9–13 feet (2.7–4 m)
Fact: Deinonychus is a fast-moving dinosaur with curved claws for killing.

CRETACEOUS PERIOD
(145-65 MYA CONTINUED)

112-90 mya

Giganotosaurus
(JEE-guh-NO-toe-SORE-us)
Family: Carcharodontosauridae
Fossils Found: Argentina
Diet: Carnivore; Length: 45 feet (14 m)
Fact: Giganotosaurus' skull is about
6 feet (1.8 m) long.

113-91 mya

Carnotaurus (KAR-nuh-TORE-us)
Family: Abelisauridae
Fossils Found: Argentina
Diet: Carnivore; Length: 25 feet (7.6 m)
Fact: Carnotaurus' name means "meat-eating bull."
Its horns look like those of a bull.

110 mya

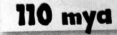

Sauroposeidon (SORE-oh-poh-SYE-don)
Family: Brachiosauridae
Fossils Found: United States
Diet: Herbivore; Length: 60 feet (18 m)
Fact: *Sauroposeidon* means "lizard earthquake
god" because the ground probably trembles
when it walks.

95-70 mya

Spinosaurus (SPY-nuh-SORE-us)
Family: Spinosauridae
Fossils Found: Egypt and Morocco
Diet: Carnivore; Length: 50 feet (15 m)
Fact: Spinosaurus has a sail on its back that may have been used to attract other dinosaurs.

85-80 mya

Protoceratops (PROH-toe-SAIR-uh-tops)
Family: Protoceratopsidae
Fossils Found: Mongolia
Diet: Herbivore; Length: 6 feet (1.8 m)
Fact: Protoceratops may have traveled in herds to protect themselves from predators.

90 mya

Argentinosaurus
(AR-gen-TEEN-uh-SORE-us)
Family: Titanosauridae
Fossils Found: Argentina
Diet: Herbivore; Length: 120 feet (37 m)
Fact: Argentinosaurus is as long as three school buses and weighs 100 tons (91 t)! It's the largest animal to walk on land.

CRETACEOUS PERIOD
(145-65 MYA CONTINUED)

83-65 mya

Lambeosaurus (LAM-bee-uh-SORE-us)
Family: Hadrosauridae
Fossils Found: United States and Canada
Diet: Herbivore
Length: Up to 49 feet (15 m)
Fact: Lambeosaurus has a bony crest
that may be used to make sounds.

78-74 mya

Hadrosaurus (HAD-ruh-SORE-us)
Family: Hadrosauridae
Fossils Found: United States
Diet: Herbivore; Length: 30 feet (9.1 m)
Fact: Unearthed in 1858, Hadrosaurus
is the first nearly complete dinosaur
fossil to be discovered in North America.

84-80 mya

Velociraptor (vel-OSS-ih-RAP-tor)
Family: Dromaeosauridae
Fossils Found: Russia and China
Diet: Carnivore; Length: 6 feet (1.8 m)
Fact: A famous Velociraptor fossil
found in 1971 shows the dinosaur
fighting a Protoceratops.

76-74 mya

Edmontonia (ED-mon-TOH-nee-uh)
Family: Nodosauridae
Fossils Found: United States and Canada
Diet: Herbivore; Length: 20 feet (6.1 m)
Fact: Edmontonia has bony neck plates, spikes
on its back and tail, and scales across its head.

76-74 mya

Chasmosaurus (KAZ-muh-SORE-us)
Family: Ceratopsidae
Fossils Found: United States and Canada
Diet: Herbivore; Length: 16 feet (4.9 m)
Fact: Chasmosaurus' neck frill may
be used to attract mates.

76-65 mya

Parasaurolophus (PAR-uh-SORE-uh-LOH-fus)
Family: Hadrosauridae
Fossils Found: United States and Canada
Diet: Herbivore; Length: 33 feet (10 m)
Fact: Parasaurolophus' crest is most likely used
to make warning sounds or to attract mates.

76-74 mya

Dromaeosaurus (DROH-mee-uh-SORE-us)
Family: Dromaeosauridae
Fossils Found: United States and Canada
Diet: Carnivore
Length: 5.5 feet (1.7 m)
Fact: Dromaeosaurus uses its
sharp claws to slash prey.

76-70 mya

Styracosaurus (stye-RAK-uh-SORE-us)
Family: Ceratopsidae
Fossils Found: United States and Canada
Diet: Herbivore; Length: 17 feet (5.2 m)
Fact: Styracosaurus' large frill may be used
for defense or to help control body temperature.

21

CRETACEOUS PERIOD
(145–65 MYA CONTINUED)

76–65 mya

Pachycephalosaurus (PACK-i-SEF-uh-luh-SORE-us)
Family: Pachycephalosauridae
Fossils Found: United States, Canada, and Mongolia
Diet: Herbivore
Length: Up to 26 feet (7.9 m)
Fact: With its domed skull, Pachycephalosaurus may fend off predators.

74–67 mya

Ankylosaurus (ang-KYE-luh-SORE-us)
Family: Ankylosauridae
Fossils Found: United States and Canada
Diet: Herbivore; Length: Up to 23 feet (7 m)
Fact: Ankylosaurus most likely uses its large round tail club to clobber predators.

76–65 mya

Stegoceras (steh-GOSS-uh-rus)
Family: Pachycephalosauridae
Fossils Found: United States and Canada
Diet: Herbivore; Length: 8 feet (2.4 m)
Fact: Stegoceras may use its domed skull to head-butt other dinosaurs.

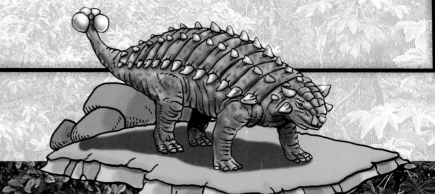

74-65 mya

Ornithomimus (OR-ni-thuh-MYE-mus)
Family: Ornithomimidae
Fossils Found: United States and Mongolia
Diet: Omnivore; Length: 11 feet (3.4 m)
Fact: Ornithomimus can possibly run
as fast as 40 miles (64 km) per hour.

67-65 mya

Triceratops (try-SAIR-uh-tops)
Family: Ceratopsidae
Fossils Found: United States and Canada
Diet: Herbivore
Length: 30 feet (9.1 m)
Fact: With its horns, Triceratops may
attract mates or battle other Triceratops.

70 mya

Troödon (TROH-uh-don)
Family: Troödontidae
Fossils Found: United States
and Canada
Diet: Carnivore
Length: Up to 6 feet (1.8 m)
Fact: Troödon is
thought to be one of
the smartest dinosaurs.

65 mya
Dinosaurs become extinct after
a possible asteroid crash causes
climate changes, disease, or
volcanic activity.

67-65 mya

Tyrannosaurus rex (tie-RAN-uh-SORE-us REX)
Family: Tyrannosauridae
Fossils Found: United States, Canada,
and Mongolia
Diet: Carnivore; Length: 40 feet (12 m)
Fact: Tyrannosaurus rex has teeth up to
9 inches (23 cm) long. It can eat 500 pounds
(227 kg) of meat in a single bite!

23

EARLY DINOSAUR DISCOVERIES

1822

Dr. Gideon Mantell and his wife find bones and teeth in England. Two years later, Dr. Mantell names the animal Iguanodon.

1824

Reverend William Buckland writes about Megalosaurus in a scientific journal.

1842

British citizen Sir Richard Owen coins the word "dinosaur."

1854

Ferdinand Vandiveer Hayden finds the first North American dinosaur remains. The collection of teeth belongs to the Trachodon, Troödon, and Deinodon dinosaurs.

1856

Joseph Leidy publishes the first description of dinosaurs in the United States. He names Trachodon, Troödon, and Deinodon.

1870s

Edward Drinker Cope and Othniel C. Marsh start the "Bone Wars," a competition of dinosaur fossil discoveries.

1858

Scientists discover some dinosaurs walked on two legs instead of four.

1858

William Parker Foulke discovers the first complete dinosaur skeleton, called Hadrosaurus.

Welcome to Haddonfield

1877

Arthur Lakes discovers giant dinosaur fossil beds in Morrison, Colorado.

DINOSAUR RUSH

1888

John Bell Hatcher finds the first nearly complete fossil of a Triceratops in Wyoming.

1897

Barnum Brown begins his career as a fossil hunter with the American Museum of Natural History. He will be considered one of the greatest fossil hunters of all time.

1879

Othniel C. Marsh coins the word "Brontosaurus" when he mistakenly gives the name to a dinosaur that has already been discovered.

1896

Andrew Carnegie opens the Carnegie Museum of Natural History in Pittsburgh, Pennsylvania. Three years later, he hires fossil-hunters to find dinosaur bones for the museum.

1902

Barnum Brown discovers the first fossils of a Tyrannosaurus rex in Montana.

1908

George Sternberg discovers an impression of an Edmontosaurus' skin in rock in Wyoming.

1909–1923

Earl Douglass removes 350 tons (318 t) of dinosaur bones from Dinosaur National Monument in Colorado and Utah.

1909

A Brachiosaurus skeleton is discovered in Tanzania. It is four stories tall and 74 feet (23 m) long.

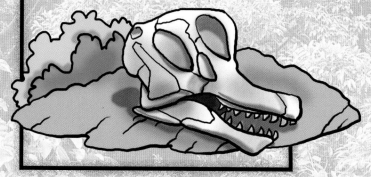

1910

In Alberta, Canada, a "dinosaur rush" begins between Barnum Brown and Charles H. Sternberg when several dinosaur fossils are found in the area.

MODERN DISCOVERIES

1947

Edwin H. Colbert discovers hundreds of Coelophysis skeletons in Ghost Ranch, New Mexico.

1972

James A. Jensen discovers one of the world's longest dinosaurs, Supersaurus, in Colorado.

1920s

Roy Chapman Andrews discovers the first fossilized dinosaur eggs. He also discovers fossils of Velociraptor.

1980

Luis Alvarez and his son Walter publicly announce evidence that the dinosaur extinction was the result of an asteroid crashing into Earth.

Sue Hendrickson unearths a nearly complete Tyrannosaurus rex skeleton in South Dakota. The skeleton is named Sue.

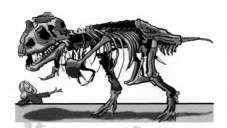

2011

Scientists announce the fossil discovery of a new species of dinosaur at Ghost Ranch in New Mexico. They name it Daemonosaurus.

2004

Scientists in China find a skeleton of one adult Psittacosaurus guarding 34 young Psittacosaurus.

1978

John R. Horner discovers Maiasaura nesting grounds in Montana.

2002

Xu Xing and his team discover the four-winged dinosaur Microraptor in China.

2006

The dinosaur Dracorex hogwartsia is named for the wizard school in the Harry Potter books. It may actually be a Pachycephalosaurus.

1995

The first dinosaur fossil with feathers, Sinosauropteryx, is discovered in China.

BUILD YOUR OWN TIMELINE

Paleontologists, "fossil hunters," get to travel around the world making discoveries. They use the newest technology and work with some of the best museums in the world. They have a very exciting job!

This book shows you the history of dinosaur discoveries and gives you a glimpse of some new ones. Create a timeline based on dinosaur discoveries happening today. Start with the last date on this book's timeline and take it to present day. You can use the references on page 31 of this book to get you started!

2011

?

?

Today

?

Glossary

armor—bones, scales, and skin covering a body

asteroid—a large space rock that moves around the sun; asteroids are too small to be called planets

carnivore—an animal that eats only meat

climate—average weather throughout the year

crest—a curved bony growth

extinct—no longer living; an extinct animal is one that has died out, with no more of its kind

fossil—the remains or traces of an animal or a plant, preserved as rock

frill—a bony collar

herbivore—an animal that eats only plants

impression—a mark or design left by pressing or stamping

mate—one of a pair

membrane—a thin, flexible layer of skin

omnivore—an animal that eats plants and other animals

Pangea—a possible continent that included all of the landmass on Earth prior to the Triassic period, when it split apart

plate—a flat, bony growth

predator—an animal that hunts animals for food

reptile—a cold-blooded animal that breathes air and has a backbone; most reptiles have scales

sail—a tall, thin, upright structure on the backs of some dinosaurs

skeleton—the bones that support and protect the body

species—a group of animals with similar features

spine—a hard, sharp, pointed growth

stud—a bony bump

vertebrate—an animal with a backbone

TO LEARN MORE

More Books to Read

Green, Jen, Dr. *The Dinosaur Museum*. Washington, D.C.: National Geographic Society, 2008.

Olien, Rebecca. *How Do We Know About Dinosaurs?: A Fossil Mystery*. Science Mysteries. Mankato, Minn.: Capstone Press, 2012.

Rissman, Rebecca. *What Were Dinosaurs?* Acorn Read Aloud. Chicago: Heinenmann Library, 2010.

Internet Sites

FactHound offers a safe, fun way to find Internet sites related to this book. All of the sites on FactHound have been researched by our staff.

Here's all you do:

Visit *www.facthound.com*

Type in this code: 9781404871625

Super-cool stuff!

Check out projects, games and lots more at
www.capstonekids.com

INDEX

Look for all the books in the series:

An Illustrated Timeline of Dinosaurs
An Illustrated Timeline of Inventions and Inventors
An Illustrated Timeline of Space Exploration

An Illustrated Timeline of Transportation
An Illustrated Timeline of U.S. Presidents
An Illustrated Timeline of U.S. States